Other books written by Kate Klise
and illustrated by M. Sarah Klise:

Over My Dead Body

Regarding the Fountain
Regarding the Sink
Regarding the Trees
Regarding the Bathrooms
Regarding the Bees

Letters from Camp
Trial by Journal
Stand Straight, Ella Kate

Shall I Knit You a Hat?
Why Do You Cry?
Imagine Harry
Little Rabbit and the Night Mare
Little Rabbit and the Meanest Mother on Earth

Also written by Kate Klise:

Deliver Us from Normal
Far from Normal

43 Old Cemetery Road: Book One

DYING TO MEET YOU

Kate

Illustrated By

Sarah Klise

sandpiper

Houghton Mifflin Harcourt
Boston New York

ACKNOWLEDGMENTS

The author and illustrator would like to thank the children
at the Wright County Children's Home
in Norwood, Missouri,
and at the Chinatown YMCA and Cameron House
in San Francisco, California,
for providing the inspiration for this book.

Text copyright © 2009 by Kate Klise
Illustrations copyright © 2009 by M. Sarah Klise

www.hmhbooks.com

The Library of Congress has cataloged the hardcover edition as follows:
Klise, Kate.
Dying to meet you: 43 Old Cemetery Road: Book one/Kate Klise; illustrated by M. Sarah Klise.
p.cm.
Summary: In this story told mostly through letters, a children's book author I. B. Grumply gets more
than he bargained for when he rents a quiet place to write for the summer.
ISBN: 978-0-15-205727-5 hardcover
ISBN: 978-0-547-39848-8 paperback
[1. Authors—Fiction. 2. Authorship—Fiction. 3. Dwellings—Fiction. 4. Haunted houses—Fiction. 5.
Ghosts—Fiction. 7. Humorous stories.] I. Klise, M. Sarah, ill. II. Title. III. Title: Dying to Meet You.
PZ7.K684Aai 2009
[Fic]—dc22 2007028534

Manufactured in the United States of America
DOC 10 9 8
4500314134

The following is a collection of
actual letters and documents
written over the course of
one summer
and pertaining to
the strange events
that took place
in a certain house
located at
43 Old Cemetery Road
in an otherwise
quiet town
called
Ghastly, Illinois.

For your convenience,
the people involved
in the events
described in
this book
are pictured here:

Ignatius B. Grumply

A famous
author
of children's
books

Anita Sale

A real estate agent

E. Gadds

Paige
Turner

The publisher
of
Grumply's books

Grumply's lawyer

A married
couple
who study
paranormal
activity

Professors Les and Diane Hope

Seymour Hope

Their 11-year-old son
and his cat, Shadow

Frank N. Beans

A private investigator

And, of course,

The woman
who built the house
at 43 Old Cemetery Road

(She died 97 years
before this story opens.)

Olive C. Spence

By turning this page

and the pages that follow,

you hereby release

the compilers of this correspondence

from all liability

related to thoughts,

ruminations,

hallucinations,

and dreams

(good or bad)

of or pertaining to

ghosts,

friendly or otherwise.

(Just trying to warn you.)

This true story begins with a letter,
which is printed in its entirety
on the next page.

IGNATIUS B. GRUMPLY

SPECIALIZING IN MYSTERIES, MAYHEM & THE MACABRE

400 SOUTH STATE STREET, APT. 2-B   CHICAGO, ILLINOIS 60605

May 22

Proper Properties
100 Larkin Street
San Francisco, CA 94102

Sir or Madam:

Is it true that you rent houses for the summer? If so, send me a list of your available properties.

I am looking for a quiet place to rent this summer while I finish writing my next children's book. (Truth is, I haven't started the book yet. But don't tell my publisher.)

Kindly respond by letter as I have disconnected all my phones. You can't imagine how pesky publishers can be when an author is late on a book deadline. They're as bad as annoying children.

Speaking of which, the house I rent *must* sit at a comfortable distance from all schools, parks, and other places where children gather. I happen to write books for children. That doesn't mean I want to see or hear the little monsters when I'm trying to work.

Cordially,

I. B. Grumply

I. B. Grumply

9.

PROPER PROPERTIES

100 Larkin Street
San Francisco, CA 94102

May 26

Mr. Ignatius B. Grumply
400 South State St., Apt 2-B
Chicago, IL 60605

Dear Mr. Grumply,

What a thrill to receive a letter from you. I
didn't even know you were still alive!

I am a HUGE fan of your books. I read all the
Ghost Tamer books when I was a little girl. My
favorite was *Bartholomew Brown: Have You
Met the Ghost Tamer?* I read it three times!

You'll be pleased to know that we have a
variety of rentals available this summer. I have
enclosed a brochure.

Please let me know if any of these properties
appeals to you. If so, I can provide more
details and arrange a tour of the property.

We never want our clients to be disappointed or surprised.

Sincerely,

Anita Sale

Anita Sale

P.S. I just can't *wait* to read your next book. Goodness, how long has it been since you wrote a new book?

Summer Rentals Available

Cape Cod cottage
Ocean views

London flat
Located near theatres

Bay Area beauty
Urban sophistication

New Listings!

from PROPER PROPERTIES

CLASSIC COTSWOLD
Charm in the
English countryside

HAMPTONS HIDEAWAY
See and be seen at
this chic retreat!

Need a House?
Call Anita Sale
1-555-REALST8

VICTORIAN LADY
32½-room mansion
43 Old Cemetery Road
Ghastly, Illinois

IGNATIUS B. GRUMPLY

SPECIALIZING IN MYSTERIES, MAYHEM & THE MACABRE

400 SOUTH STATE STREET, APT. 2-B   CHICAGO, ILLINOIS 60605

OVERNIGHT MAIL

May 29

Ms. Anita Sale
Proper Properties
100 Larkin Street
San Francisco, CA 94102

Ms. Sale:

I'll take it. I shall move into the house on Old Cemetery Road this weekend.

Send a rental contract to my attorney, E. Gadds. He handles all such paperwork for me.

For your information, it's been 20 years since I wrote a Ghost Tamer book. But I hardly see how that's any of *your* business.

Cordially,

I. B. Grumply

I. B. Grumply

CC: E. Gadds, Attorney-at-Law
        188 Madison Avenue
        New York, NY 10016

Gadds: Sign whatever Ms. Sale sends
and remit full payment for the summer.
                      -IBG

PROPER PROPERTIES

Elegant Estates   Historic Homes   Classic Cottages

100 Larkin Street
San Francisco, CA 94102

OVERNIGHT MAIL

May 30

Mr. Ignatius B. Grumply
400 South State St., Apt. 2-B
Chicago, IL 60605

Dear Mr. Grumply,

Thank you for your quick response. I appreciate your enthusiasm, but I must tell you: The
house at 43 Old Cemetery Road is *not* a property I would recommend for you.

The owners of this house have been trying
to sell it for years. No one wants to buy it
because . . . Oh, it's a long, silly story!

I *did* send a rental contract to your attorney, as
you instructed. But I really think you would

be much happier somewhere else. May I suggest a *très* charming apartment in Paris instead? Or a rustic farmhouse in Tuscany?

I will enclose some new listings with this letter.

Sincerely,

Anita Sale

Anita Sale

TO:

Mr. Ignatius B. Grumply
400 South State St.
    Apt. 2-B
Chicago, IL 60605

-Seymour Hope

O.C.S.

Sunday, June 1

Dearest Seymour,

There's no need for you to be rude
to our new guest.

That's *my* job, remember?

Love,

Olive

June 1

Hi, Olive!

Sorry. I didn't mean to be rude. But I don't
like this guy already. Can't you get rid of him,
like you did the others?

Please????

   —Seymour

O.C.S.

Sunday, June 1

Seymour,

I plan on it, dear.

But let me have a little fun with him first. This one looks interesting.

Love,

Olive

⇜THE GHASTLY TIMES⇝

Sunday, June 1
Cliff Hanger, Editor

"Your Secrets Are Our Business"

$1.50
☀ Morning Edition

Famous Author to Live in Ghastly This Summer

Ignatius B. Grumply, 64, author of the popular Ghost Tamer series of children's books, will spend the summer right here in Ghastly.

Grumply is renting the house at 43 Old Cemetery Rd., known locally as Spence Mansion. (See story below.)

The house, owned by Professors Les and Diane Hope, is for sale.

"The Hopes are offering their house for rent until a buyer can be found," said Anita Sale of Proper Properties.

Grumply is renting local mansion.

Grumply declined requests for interviews with a gruff "Go away!"

"He's working on a new book in the Ghost Tamer series, and he doesn't want to be bothered," explained Sale in a phone interview from her office in California.

"Personally," continued Sale, "I think Ignatius Grumply is an old grouchypants, but don't print that in the newspaper."

(Sorry, Anita. Your secrets are our business!)

Spence Mansion Built on the Hope of a Writer Who Died a Failure

Olive C. Spence's parties at her mansion were legendary.

It seems only fitting that Ignatius B. Grumply should rent Spence Mansion. After all, the Victorian house was built in 1874 by the late Olive C. Spence as a place to write.

Spence wrote and illustrated dozens of mysteries while living in her three-story house. She threw elaborate parties for the whole town to celebrate the completion of her manuscripts.

But much to her frustration, Spence could never find a publisher willing to buy her graphic mysteries, which were undoubtedly ahead of their time.

Those who knew Spence say the continual rejection caused her to withdraw

(Continued on page 2, column 1)

MANSION *(Continued from page 1, column 2)*

from society. In her final years, Spence, who never married or had children, rarely left the mansion. Her death 97 years ago was attributed to a heart broken by her failed literary career.

Legend has it that shortly before her death, Spence vowed to haunt her house and the town of Ghastly for eternity or until one of her mysteries was published, whichever came first.

"That's a lot of hogwash," said Mac Awbrah, owner of Ghastly Antiques. Over the years Spence's image has reportedly appeared in an old mirror in the antique shop. Attempts to photograph the image have failed.

"If people want to believe in ghosts, let 'em," continued Awbrah. "I certainly don't."

Nor does Barry A. Lyve, owner of Ghastly Pet Store, where a 197-year-old giant tortoise named Mr. Poe curls its mouth into a sly smile whenever anyone mentions Spence's name.

But at the Ghastly Gourmand, owner Shirley U. Jest has given up baking peach pies.

"I'm told it was Olive's favorite dessert," said Jest. "Now I'm not saying I believe in ghosts. I'm just saying every time I bake a peach pie, the dang thing disappears from the cooling rack. Same with chocolate-chip muffins."

Les and Diane Hope were well aware of the history of Spence Mansion when they purchased the house 12 years ago after it had sat empty for more than eight decades. As professors of the paranormal, the Hopes had hoped to study and document the ghost of Olive C. Spence.

"If we can get Olive's ghost to perform, we'll make a fortune," Les Hope said the day he and his wife moved into the house.

"We'll be the richest professors of the

The Hopes hoped to profit from their ghostly research in Ghastly.

paranormal in America," Diane Hope added. "Maybe the whole world!"

But when repeated experiments failed to detect any evidence of ghosts in Spence Mansion, Les and Diane Hope put the house up for sale. They are spending the summer on a tour of Europe, promoting their research conclusions in a lecture entitled "Only Fools (and Children) Believe in Ghosts."

The Hopes left their only child, Seymour, behind for professional reasons.

Library Books Missing (Again)

A dozen children's books are missing from the Ghastly Public Library.

"I really don't understand it," said M. Balm, chief librarian. "Anyone with a library card can borrow books for free. There's no reason to steal them. I'm asking whoever took the books to please return them."

M. Balm requests return of stolen books.

The 12 missing books are from the Ghost Tamer series by Ignatius B. Grumply.

This is not the first time the Ghastly Public Library has had a problem with stolen books or mysterious phenomena.

"But let's not get into all that, OK?" begged Balm.

IGNATIUS B. GRUMPLY

SPECIALIZING IN MYSTERIES, MAYHEM & THE MACABRE

TEMPORARY ADDRESS

43 OLD CEMETERY ROAD   **GHASTLY, ILLINOIS**

OVERNIGHT MAIL

June 2

Ms. Anita Sale
Proper Properties
100 Larkin Street
San Francisco, CA 94102

Ms. Sale:

There is a serious problem with the house I've
rented. *A young boy is living on the third floor.*

I encountered him for the first time this morning
when I was familiarizing myself with the house.
The boy was in a tiny room on the third floor
that can be reached only by climbing the most
perilous staircase and then creeping down a
crooked hallway. The entire house is arranged
in this same higgledy-piggledy style. Whoever
designed it must've been half batty.

But back to the child: He was sitting on a bed and drawing in a notebook. When I asked his name, he turned briefly to look at me. Then he resumed sketching.

I suspect this boy is responsible for the *anti-*welcome party that greeted my arrival to this hapless hamlet. But never mind that.

I am asking that you have this child removed from the house <u>immediately</u>.

Also, there is a cat in the house. *I am highly allergic to cats. The cat must be removed, too.*

You may respond by letter. I have disconnected phone service to this house in order to minimize distractions to my writing.

Yours in crisis,

I. B. Grumply

I. B. Grumply

100 Larkin Street
San Francisco, CA 94102

June 3

Mr. Ignatius B. Grumply
43 Old Cemetery Road
Ghastly, Illinois

Dear Mr. Grumply,

If you had read the rental agreement, you would have seen the following clause:

> **CLAUSE 102 (a): Seymour Hope will be allowed to remain at 43 Old Cemetery Road. Whoever rents the property will care for Seymour and his cat, Shadow, for the duration of the rental agreement, and return them both in healthy condition to Les and Diane Hope, if they so request.**

You asked me to send the contract to your lawyer, E. Gadds, who signed on your behalf and sent full payment for the summer rental.

I then forwarded that money, minus my commission, to Les and Diane Hope. (They're Seymour's parents.)

I'm sorry you're unhappy about your housemates. But I *did* try to warn you.

Good luck with your book.

Sincerely,

Anita Sale

Anita Sale

P.S. Spence Mansion was designed by a woman named Olive C. Spence. Like you, Ms. Spence was a writer, though her books were never published. Maybe you'll find one of her mysteries tucked away somewhere in the house. Could be fun!

IGNATIUS B. GRUMPLY

SPECIALIZING IN MYSTERIES, MAYHEM & THE MACABRE

TEMPORARY ADDRESS

43 OLD CEMETERY ROAD

GHASTLY, ILLINOIS

June 5

Ms. Anita Sale
Proper Properties
100 Larkin Street
San Francisco, CA 94102

Ms. Sale:

I have no interest in finding and/or reading the work of a woman who, judging from her publishing failures, knew as little about writing books as she did about designing houses.

My next letter will be to my lawyer, who I'm sure will clear up this matter of my unwanted housemates.

Yours with a handkerchief held to my nose,

I. B. Grumply

I. B. Grumply

IGNATIUS B. GRUMPLY

SPECIALIZING IN MYSTERIES, MAYHEM & THE MACABRE

TEMPORARY ADDRESS

43 OLD CEMETERY ROAD   GHASTLY, ILLINOIS

<u>OVERNIGHT MAIL</u>

June 5

E. Gadds
Attorney-at-Law
188 Madison Avenue
New York, NY 10016

Gadds:

You've gotten me into a fine pickle now. I
wanted to rent a house somewhere quiet for
the summer. I'd hoped a change of location
would help me write the 13th book in that
blasted Ghost Tamer series.

Instead, I find myself in a creaky old house
held together by the faintest whisper of paint.
Worse yet, I'm sharing this hovel with a
young boy and his cat.

Why would the parents of this child leave him in *my* care? I don't even *like* children. And I despise cats.

Never mind that. Whatever you signed to get me into this mess, *un*sign it. I don't care what it costs. Just get me out of this backwater dump—*NOW*.

Your unhappiest client,

Ignatius

Ignatius B. Grumply

E. GADDS

ATTORNEY-AT-LAW
188 MADISON AVENUE
NEW YORK, NEW YORK 10016

EXPRESS MAIL

June 6

Ignatius B. Grumply
43 Old Cemetery Road
Ghastly, Illinois

Dear Ignatius,

I needed a laugh this morning. Thank you!

But really, you can't instruct me in one letter to sign a contract and then, in the next letter, tell me to *un*sign it. That is a binding rental agreement.

As for the money, maybe *you* don't care about it, but I do. Ignatius, do you realize that you are flat broke? Actually, you're much worse than broke, because you now owe me $3,000 for this flophouse you've rented for the summer. And, you've already spent the $100,000 advance you received for the new Ghost Tamer book, which you *still* haven't written.

Paige Turner called here yesterday to ask if I knew where you—and more important, your next book—were. Did you forget to tell your publisher that you were leaving town? I covered for you, Ignatius, but I can't keep this up. She said you're already two months late on your deadline.

Find a quiet room in that house and write the next Ghost Tamer book. I'm going to repeat that, Ignatius: *Write. The. Next. Ghost. Tamer. Book.* You need the money. Your bad investments and lavish lifestyle have made you a very poor man.

Sincerely,

E. Gadds

E. Gadds

P.S. Just so you know, you're obligated to care for Seymour Hope and his cat until September 1, as per the rental contract. Who knows? Maybe the boy will provide some necessary inspiration. You need something (or someone) to help cure your writer's block.

IGNATIUS B. GRUMPLY

SPECIALIZING IN MYSTERIES, MAYHEM & THE MACABRE

TEMPORARY ADDRESS

43 OLD CEMETERY ROAD   GHASTLY, ILLINOIS

June 7

E. Gadds
Attorney-at-Law
188 Madison Avenue
New York, NY 10016

Gadds:

Thanks for nothing.

If Turner calls again, tell her I'll have the book
finished by August 1.

Ignatius
Ignatius B. Grumply

P.S. I do *not* have writer's block. I just haven't
felt like writing for a few years. (Okay, a few
decades.) I still don't feel like writing, but I'm
going to start now if for no other reason than to
get you and Paige Turner off my back.

Book #13 in the Ghost Tamer series

Mystery at Old Cemetery Road:
Bartholomew Brown Returns!

Chapter One

The house was old and creaky. Had he
known exactly *how* old and creaky, Bartholomew
Brown would never have rented it for the summer.

But rent it he had. And so, the famous
ghost detective proposed to make the best of it.

"I suppose I can tame ghosts here as well as
anywhere," Brown sighed as he stood on the front
porch of the house and unfurled a tattered flag. It
was the same flag Brown flew wherever he worked:
a simple gray canvas with these words printed
tastefully in heather blue: *Bartholomew Brown:*
Ghost Tamer (Inquire Within).

~~The next day, Bartholomew Brown . . .~~
~~He . . . It . . . The . . .~~
~~When . . .~~

ACK! It's *impossible* to write with all of
these distractions!!!!

IGNATIUS B. GRUMPLY

SPECIALIZING IN MYSTERIES, MAYHEM & THE MACABRE

TEMPORARY ADDRESS

43 OLD CEMETERY ROAD   GHASTLY, ILLINOIS

June 8

Seymour Hope
Third floor
43 Old Cemetery Road
Ghastly, Illinois

Seymour:

Because of a grievous oversight on my part,
it appears we will be spending the summer
together. As such, I wish to establish a few
house rules.

HOUSE RULES

Rule 1: You will not bother me when I am
writing.

Rule 2: You will stay out of my bedroom and
bathroom at all times.

Rule 3: You will not lurk in doorways or dark
hallways.

Rule 4: You will not pester me with requests for autographs or signed copies of my books.

Rule 5: If we must communicate, we will do so in writing. You may leave letters for me outside my bedroom door. Otherwise, you are not permitted on the second floor* of the house, which I have claimed as my own for the duration of the summer.

If I think of additional house rules, I shall add them to the list.

From the second floor,

I. B. Grumply

I. B. Grumply

*Except as is necessary in transit to and from your quarters on the third floor.

June 9

Mr. Grumply,

I read your rules. I have a few of my own I'd like to add.

HOUSE RULES (continued)

Rule 6: You will not tell me what time I have to go to bed.

Rule 7: You will not tell me what to eat or when to eat it.

Rule 8: You will not play old man music on the stereo.

Rule 9: I won't ask for your autograph if you won't ask me to read any of your books. I've never read a Ghost Tamer book in my life. I don't really like reading. I'd rather draw.

Rule 10: You can leave letters for me outside my room. Other than that, you're not allowed on the third floor. No exceptions.

   -Seymour Hope

O.C.S.

Wednesday, June 11

Seymour,

Good job standing your ground! This
Grumply character is a piece of work—
and I don't mean *art*work.

Did you know the old coot is responsible
for those dreadful Ghost Tamer books?
I'm reading the whole series now.

Imagine: a collection of books about a
man who thinks he can tame a ghost.
What *hunk*!

Love,

Olive

IGNATIUS B. GRUMPLY

SPECIALIZING IN MYSTERIES, MAYHEM & THE MACABRE

TEMPORARY ADDRESS

43 OLD CEMETERY ROAD   GHASTLY, ILLINOIS

June 12

Seymour Hope
Third floor
43 Old Cemetery Road
Ghastly, Illinois

Seymour:

I must insist that you *not* bother me when I'm trying to write. The sound of doors slamming upstairs
is most distracting. This must stop.

Furthermore, you mentioned in your note that you
hadn't read any of my books. And yet I saw a stack
of 12 Ghost Tamer books on the dining room table
this morning when I went downstairs for breakfast.

Therefore, I am adding the following to our list of
house rules:

<u>Rule 11: No lying.</u>

Firmly,

I. B. Grumply

I. B. Grumply

June 12

Mr. Grumply,

Fine. Then I'll add this:

Rule 12: No false accusations.

I didn't lie. And those aren't my books. I suspect someone in this house has been stealing library books again.

Hello, Olive?

—Seymour Hope

IGNATIUS B. GRUMPLY

SPECIALIZING IN MYSTERIES, MAYHEM & THE MACABRE

TEMPORARY ADDRESS

43 OLD CEMETERY ROAD   **GHASTLY, ILLINOIS**

June 12

Seymour Hope
Third floor
43 Old Cemetery Road
Ghastly, Illinois

Seymour:

Now listen here, young man. I've never stolen
a library book in my life. And my name is
Ignatius, not Olive.

But I'd prefer you address me as *Mr. Grumply*
in your communiqués.

Losing my patience on the second floor,

I. B. Grumply

I. B. Grumply

June 12

Mr. Grumply,

I know what your name is. I was talking to someone else.

Her name's Olive and she lives in the cupola. That's
this part of the house:

She's a ghost and my
best friend. Sometimes
she slams doors when
she's mad. She steals
library books whenever
she wants.

I'm sure she'll introduce
herself to you when she
feels like it. Right, Olive?

    –Seymour Hope

IGNATIUS B. GRUMPLY

SPECIALIZING IN MYSTERIES, MAYHEM & THE MACABRE

TEMPORARY ADDRESS

43 OLD CEMETERY ROAD   GHASTLY, ILLINOIS

June 13

E. Gadds
Attorney-at-Law
188 Madison Avenue
New York, NY 10016

Gadds:

You'll enjoy this.

Seymour Hope, my summer housemate, is
apparently trying to scare me away by claiming
there's a ghost named Olive living in the cupola
of this hovel.

Amusing, no? The boy must take me for a fool.

I begin the book in earnest tomorrow.

Ignatius

Ignatius B. Grumply

E. GADDS

ATTORNEY-AT-LAW
188 MADISON AVENUE
NEW YORK, NEW YORK 10016

June 16

Ignatius B. Grumply
43 Old Cemetery Road
Ghastly, Illinois

Dear Ignatius,

Very comical about the kid and the "ghost." Use it in the book.

Speaking of which, your publisher called again this morning. I told her you were out of town on family business. She responded: "*What family?* Grumply doesn't have a wife or kids. I don't think he even has any friends, does he?"

I replied that I was your friend. She laughed and added: "Only because he *pays* you." (I didn't tell her that, in fact, you *owe* me money.)

Ignatius, I've been your attorney for a long time. You have no bigger fan in the world than me. But

I'm concerned. If you don't think you can write the 13th Ghost Tamer book, you must tell me now so I can start trying to wiggle out of that contract with Paige Turner Books. Turner will insist you return the $100,000 she's already paid you for this book, but we'll try to work out a payment plan—somehow.

Let me know.

E. Gadds

E. Gadds

IGNATIUS B. GRUMPLY

SPECIALIZING IN MYSTERIES, MAYHEM & THE MACABRE

TEMPORARY ADDRESS

43 OLD CEMETERY ROAD   GHASTLY, ILLINOIS

June 18

E. Gadds
Attorney-at-Law
188 Madison Avenue
New York, NY 10016

Gadds:

Thank you for running interference again with
Turner.

I have every intention of starting—and finishing—this book. I am locking myself in my room
to write as soon as I sign my name to this letter.

I'll have this book finished before you can say
"boo."

Ignatius

Ignatius B. Grumply

Book #13 in the Ghost Tamer series

Mystery at Old Cemetery Road: Bartholomew Brown Returns!

Chapter One

The house was old and creaky. Had he known exactly *how* old and creaky, Bartholomew Brown would never have rented it for the summer.

But rent it he had. And so, the famous ghost detective proposed to make the best of it.

After depositing his suitcase in the front hallway, Bartholomew set off to acquaint himself with the house that would be his home for the summer.

He began in the front parlor. A tired-looking sofa rested on one side of the room under an oil painting of a grim-faced woman.

"Now there's a face that could wake the dead," Brown said. He stood in front of the portrait, studying it, until a mouse scurried across his shoe.

He crossed the front hall and entered
a room that held only tattered furniture and
an upright piano with yellowing keys that
looked like teeth from the carcass of an ancient
beast.

~~He . . .~~

~~It . . .~~

~~The . . .~~ UGH!!!

IGNATIUS B. GRUMPLY

SPECIALIZING IN MYSTERIES, MAYHEM & THE MACABRE

TEMPORARY ADDRESS

43 OLD CEMETERY ROAD   **GHASTLY, ILLINOIS**

June 18

Seymour Hope
Third floor
43 Old Cemetery Road
Ghastly, Illinois

Seymour:

You are in violation of Rule 1, which states that
you will NOT bother me when I am writing. This
includes playing the piano. The sound of your fin-
gers banging on the keys makes my head throb.

If you *must* play the piano, do so in the afternoon,
when I take my daily walk.

I. B. Grumply

I. B. Grumply

P.S. If there is one excuse for the existence of
cats, it is for the elimination of mice. Perhaps
your cat could provide some necessary extermina-
tion services on the first floor.

52.

June 19

Mr. Grumply,

That wasn't me. I don't even know how to play the piano. But Olive's really good at it.

Have you met her yet? There she is right now! Do you hear her? She's stomping around in the cupola. She must be mad at somebody. Either that or she's lost her glasses again. That always makes her cranky.

   —Seymour Hope

P.S. Shadow doesn't like mice. He likes Olive's cooking better. She's been cooking for us every night since my parents left.

This is me watching Olive make dinner.

This is me eating dinner with Olive and Shadow.

This is me listening to Olive play the piano after dinner.

June 20

Ms. Anita Sale
Proper Properties
100 Larkin Street
San Francisco, CA 94102

Ms. Sale:

It is one thing to provide summer babysitting services for an abandoned child. It is quite another to do so for a child who suffers from hallucinations and/or is a shameless liar.

I am referring to Seymour Hope, who has informed me that a "ghost" named Olive is living in the cupola of this house, and cooking for him and his cat on a nightly basis.

Now, I am well aware that children have a strange fascination with the macabre. I have made (and lost) a fortune due to this very fact.

But Ms. Sale, this Hope boy is stomping around in the cupola, slamming doors, stealing library books, *and* banging on a tuneless piano at midnight, thereby distracting me from writing my next book, <u>which is why I rented this so-called Victorian lady in the first place.</u>

If you won't refund my rent, you can at least tell me how and where to contact the boy's parents. Their son clearly needs professional help. I intend to inform them of such, if you will promptly send me their summer address.

Responsibly,

I. B. Grumply

I. B. Grumply

100 Larkin Street
San Francisco, CA 94102

June 23

Mr. Ignatius B. Grumply
43 Old Cemetery Road
Ghastly, Illinois

Dear Mr. Grumply,

I *do* have an address for Les and Diane Hope. In
fact, I am the only person who knows where they
are during their lecture tour. But I'm afraid I can't
share that information with you. I'm under strict
orders *not* to contact them unless I have a buyer for
their house.

Regarding Seymour: I'm afraid I know *all* about
him. That boy has successfully scared away every
prospective renter *and* buyer I've found for Spence
Mansion with his "ghost" stories and imitations.
He even wrote me a letter last month, telling me
how he planned to buy the house himself. "I happen to like living here with Olive," Seymour wrote.
"I'm the only person who can see her, but only
when she *wants* to be seen, which isn't all that

often. Olive likes her privacy. And she doesn't like people who try to make money off her, like my parents wanted to do."

Of course Seymour needs professional help. But I'm afraid I can't share his parents' summer address with you—unless *you're* interested in buying Spence Mansion. If so, I'd be happy to put you in touch with Les and Diane Hope!

If it's any comfort, there's no need to worry about a ghost in Spence Mansion. Les and Diane Hope are world-famous professors of the paranormal. They bought the house at 43 Old Cemetery Road actually *hoping* to find a ghost but couldn't. What they discovered instead was that their son was even more delusional than they thought.

Now can you understand why Professors Les and Diane Hope didn't want their son to go to Europe with them? He's a very sick boy, and his silly shenanigans threaten to undermine his parents' research findings—not to mention *my* ability to sell Spence Mansion.

Sincerely,

Anita Sale

Anita Sale

P.S. How's the book coming along? I hope it's not unlucky to write the 13th book in a series.

IGNATIUS B. GRUMPLY

SPECIALIZING IN MYSTERIES, MAYHEM & THE MACABRE

TEMPORARY ADDRESS

43 OLD CEMETERY ROAD   **GHASTLY, ILLINOIS**

June 26

Ms. Anita Sale
Proper Properties
100 Larkin Street
San Francisco, CA 94102

Ms. Sale:

Me—interested in buying this old rattrap? I hardly think so.

Nor am I frightened by schoolyard rumors and/or cheap imitations of ghosts. Why? For the simple reason, Ms. Sale, that there are *no such things as ghosts*.

Your staggering unwillingness to be of assistance is matched only by your stultifying ignorance.

I. B. Grumply
I. B. Grumply

P.S. Only illiterate imbeciles such as yourself believe in black magic and unlucky numbers. For your information, and despite the abysmal conditions under which I am working, the book is coming along just fine. I shall resume my work on it as soon as I post this letter.

Mystery at Old Cemetery Road:
Bartholomew Brown Returns!

Chapter One

The house was old and creaky. Had he known exactly *how* old and creaky, Bartholomew Brown would never have rented it for the summer.

But rent it he had. And so, the famous ghost detective proposed to make the best of it.

He decided the situation called for a nice meal in a fine dining establishment. He hadn't eaten since very early in the day, and his appetite was keen. Nobody relished the anticipation of a good meal like Bartholomew Brown.

But just as he reached for his hat and linen jacket, a mongrel cat crept in his room with a baked chicken thigh, dripping with cream sauce, dangling from its feral jaws.

Bartholomew Brown's appetite evaporated.

"This," he sighed, "could be a very long summer."

O.C.S.

Thursday, June 26

My sentiments exactly.

But it's still boring. Your book,
I mean. I read it while you were
taking a walk.

Olive

IGNATIUS B. GRUMPLY

SPECIALIZING IN MYSTERIES, MAYHEM & THE MACABRE

TEMPORARY ADDRESS

43 OLD CEMETERY ROAD   GHASTLY, ILLINOIS

June 26

Seymour Hope
Third floor
43 Old Cemetery Road
Ghastly, Illinois

Seymour:

You little twit. How dare you call my work in
progress *boring*? And what were you doing in
my room?

If you continue to violate the established house
rules, I shall have to punish you.

Oh, very clever. Slamming doors again, are we?
While playing the piano. I believe I know a young
boy who needs a spanking.

On my way to the third floor,

I. B. Grumply

I. B. Grumply

O.C.S.

Thursday, June 26

If you lay one hand on that boy,
you will regret it.

Olive

July 1

E. Gadds
Attorney-at-Law
188 Madison Avenue
New York, NY 10016

Gadds:

I'm writing this from the hospital. Don't worry.
The emergency has passed and I am still alive,
if somewhat shaken.

It was the strangest thing. On Thursday night
of last week at approximately seven o'clock, I
was marching down the second-floor hallway on
my way to talk some sense, in the form of a
spanking, into my 11-year-old housemate, when
a crystal chandelier came crashing down from
the ceiling.

It missed me—but only by a matter of inches.
I couldn't avoid stepping on several shards of
glass, which punctured my Italian slippers.

Hence the four stitches in my left foot and six stitches in my right.

But here's the oddest part: Minutes before this happened, the boy, who's still trying to scare me with his "ghost" imitations, slipped a note under my door, telling me that I would regret laying as much as one hand on him.

That is, I *think* it was the boy. I didn't actually *see* him slip the note under my door—or even write it, for that matter. If I didn't know better, I might think . . .

Never mind. This whole situation is completely preposterous. And yes, I intend to weave it *all* into the book, if I can just get a little peace and quiet so that I can *write*.

No need to respond to this letter, Gadds. I just needed someone to talk to. I feel better already.

I shall be back at work on the book as soon as I'm released from the hospital.

With confidence and only a slight limp,

Ignatius

Ignatius B. Grumply

July 2

Hi, Olive!

Nice job getting rid of Mr. Grumply.

-Seymour

This is Mr. Grumply on his last day here.

O.C.S.

Thursday, July 3

Dear Seymour,

I'm not finished with Ignatius B. Grumply. I'm having far too much fun with this one! Plus, I'm reading his diary. It's much better than that dreary little Ghost Tamer book he's trying to write.

But never mind that. Do you really want to buy my house? If so, you're going to need a lot more money than the $36.75 you've saved from your paper route.

Why don't you mow Mrs. McCorpse's yard? I'd do it myself, but what would people say if they saw a lawn mower barreling around a yard by itself? Being invisible is frightfully convenient, but it does have its drawbacks.

If you work hard today, I'll make chicken *paprikash* for dinner Saturday night. Eight o'clock sharp. Proper attire, please.

Would you mind if I invited Mr. Grumply to dine with us?

Love,

Olive

July 3

Olive,

Why in the world do you want to invite Mr. Grumply to eat dinner with us?

I like it best when it's just you, me, and Shadow.

 —Seymour

O.C.S.

Friday, July 4

Dearest Seymour,

Why invite Grumply to dinner? Because he's enormously fun to tease. Honestly, I haven't had this much fun in 80 years.

And here he comes now in a cab! Oh heavens. Look at all those bandages. I hadn't realized how dangerous a chandelier could be.

Now I feel a twinge of guilt. I most definitely *will* invite him to dine with us. The poor fool. Just look at him hobbling up the stairs to his room. He's sitting down at his desk. Looks like he's writing a letter to you.

Oh dear. I'll let you read it yourself.

Love,

Olive

July 4

Seymour Hope
Third floor
43 Old Cemetery Road
Ghastly, Illinois

Seymour:

We seem to have gotten off on the wrong foot, as it were. But we have almost two full months left to live together under this roof. In that time, I must write a book.

As such, I am asking that you adhere to the house rules, which, in light of recent events, I am adding to as follows:

Rule 13: No reading my manuscript.

Rule 14: No causing dangerous objects (such as chandeliers) to fall from the ceiling.

I must insist on these rules so that I can work on my book, which I intend to do right now.

I. B. Grumply

I. B. Grumply

70.

Book #13 in the Ghost Tamer series

Mystery at Old Cemetery Road:
Bartholomew Brown Returns!

Chapter One

The house was old and creaky. Had he
known exactly *how* old and creaky, Bartholomew
Brown would never have rented it for the summer.

But rent it he had. And so, the famous
ghost detective proposed to make the best of it.

Bartholomew Brown picked up his suitcase
and ascended the dusty staircase to the second
floor. Walking down the long hallway, he eyed a
cobweb-laced chandelier that hung on a frayed
cord from the ceiling.

That, thought Brown, *is an accident waiting
to happen*.

As he pondered the

O.C.S.

Friday, July 4
11:45 P.M.

Ignatius,

You fell asleep at your computer. I hope you don't mind that I carried you to bed and tucked you in.

And about the chandelier: I apologize. It's been a long time since I've tackled something quite so dramatic. I'm afraid I'm a little rusty. (Well? You would be, too, if you were 190 years old.)

Now, about this book of yours: You have a decent start.

SETUP:

> Our main character is the author of a dull little series of children's books about a "ghost tamer" named Bartholomew Brown.

> This character is under contract to write a 13th book in the series, but he's stuck— both creatively and personally.

He goes to a place full of dramatic possi-
bility: a Victorian mansion.

COMPLICATIONS:
Once he arrives, the author discovers that
an 11-year-old boy will be sharing the
house with him for the summer.

The house is haunted by a *real* ghost, who
happens to be a better writer than our
main character, even if she has a short
temper. (Again, I'm sorry about the chandelier.)

But don't you see, Ignatius? Therein lies our
CONFLICT, which is at the heart of any good
story.

Now, as I see it, the setting and relationships
must connect. The mood must change.

But first I ask myself: Whose story is this?
Bartholomew Brown's? I think not. Do I care
about him as a character? Not really. He's too
flat. Too stiff. Completely unbelievable.

What about the self-absorbed author who's writing about Brown? Does this story involve him? Maybe. Or is it the glamorous ghost's story? And where does the boy fit in?

All mildly interesting, but not as intriguing as this: What will it take for our main character (the crotchety old writer) to believe in the ghost? Would an encounter help?

Let's just have a lovely dinner on Saturday night, shall we?

You know, Ignatius, if you ever bothered to get to know an actual ghost, you'd realize that we can't be *tamed,* like a dolphin or a circus lion.

Just trying to be helpful.

Olive

P.S. Oh, and happy Independence Day. Apologies in advance if I awaken you by shooting a few fireworks off the roof.

IGNATIUS B. GRUMPLY

SPECIALIZING IN MYSTERIES, MAYHEM & THE MACABRE

TEMPORARY ADDRESS

43 OLD CEMETERY ROAD   GHASTLY, ILLINOIS

July 5
1:45 A.M.

Seymour Hope
Third floor
43 Old Cemetery Road
Ghastly, Illinois

Seymour:

You are a clever boy. Of that there is little doubt.
And I give you credit for trying to run me out of
this house with your "ghost" imitations.

But the very notion of you reading my work in
progress *and* shooting fireworks off the roof All
Night Long While I Am Trying to Sleep Is
<u>Intolerable</u>.

I am calling the police right now.

I. B. Grumply
I. B. Grumply

75.

O.C.S.

Saturday, July 5
2:07 A.M.

You silly man. There's no phone
service in this house. By your choice,
remember?

Now be a good sport and join us for
dinner tonight. Eight o'clock sharp.
I'm making chicken *paprikash,* if I
can scare up the ingredients and a
recipe.

From the cupola,

Olive

➤THE GHASTLY TIMES➤

Saturday, July 5
Cliff Hanger, Editor

"Your Secrets Are Our Business"

50 cents
Afternoon Edition

Books Back but Now Chicken Missin'
Bizarre Crime Wave Rocks Ghastly

Police respond to incidents at Ghastly Grocers and the Tality house.

Chief librarian M. Balm found 12 volumes of the Ghost Tamer series on his desk this morning when he opened the Ghastly Public Library.

"But now we're missing our only Hungarian cookbook," said Balm. "I wish whoever is illegally borrowing these books would simply get a library card. It would save us all a lot of confusion."

Balm refused to speculate on whether the illegal borrowing of books might be related to the persistent legend that Olive C. Spence regularly visits the Ghastly Public Library. For decades library patrons have reported seeing pages of books turning seemingly on their own.

Meanwhile, over at Ghastly Grocers, owner Kay Daver is puzzled by the disappearance of all the paprika from her store.

"I had five jars of paprika yesterday," said Daver. "Today they're all gone."

And on the other side of town, Fay Tality has reported a package of chicken missing from her refrigerator.

"I could've sworn it was there," stated Tality. "I just bought the chicken yesterday. I was going to grill it for dinner tonight."

Police questioned everyone in the Tality household. No one had eaten the chicken, including the family dog, Mort.

Grumply's New Book Almost Done

Attention Ignatius B. Grumply fans:

The long wait is finally over. Grumply's first book in 20 years is coming out later this year.

So says Paige Turner, publisher of Paige Turner Books in New York City.

"Mr. Grumply's lawyer has promised me that Ignatius will have the new book finished by August 1," said Turner in a phone interview with *The Ghastly Times*. "That means we'll have the 13th book in the Ghost Tamer series in libraries and bookstores in time for Halloween."

Asked to describe the plot of the book, Turner said: "All I can say is that it's a mystery, even to me. I haven't seen a word of it. And frankly, I didn't know if grumpy old Grumply had another book in him. But don't print that in the paper, OK?"

(Sorry, Paige. Your secrets are our business!)

Grumply continues to refuse requests for interviews with *The Ghastly Times*. But we'll keep trying.

Bad Luck Follows Hopes on Lecture Tour

According to real estate agent Anita Sale, Les and Diane Hope are having bad luck on their lecture tour of Europe.

Les and Diane Hope, professors of paranormal activity, planned to spend the summer in Europe lecturing on their recent research findings into the "absolute impossibility of the existence of ghosts."

But the Hopes' lecture tour has been frustrated by a series of flukes, including power outages in lecture halls, flat tires on rental cars, and food poisoning.

"The Hopes have been forced to cancel all of their lectures and refund their speaking fees," said Sale, who spoke yesterday by phone with Professor Diane Hope. Les is suffering from acute laryngitis.

"Because of this setback," continued Sale, "the Hopes have agreed to reduce the price on their home at 43 Old Cemetery Road. These are very eager sellers, which is good news for anyone in the market for a house with a . . . well, er, um . . . *storied* history."

Professors Les and Diane Hope are reducing the asking price of Spence Mansion.

IGNATIUS B. GRUMPLY

SPECIALIZING IN MYSTERIES, MAYHEM & THE MACABRE
TEMPORARY ADDRESS
43 OLD CEMETERY ROAD   GHASTLY, ILLINOIS

July 6

E. Gadds
Attorney-at-Law
188 Madison Avenue
New York, NY 10016

Gadds:

I think I'm losing my mind. Let me try to explain.

Two nights ago Seymour (my housemate) slipped a letter under my door, inviting me to dinner. The letter was allegedly written by "Olive," the ghost this kid has dreamed up to try to scare me—and everyone—away from this house.

Well, I didn't make much of the invitation until last night at six o'clock, when the most enticing smells began filling the house. My curiosity got the better of me, so I hobbled downstairs on my crutches to the dining room, where I found a tantalizing dinner awaiting.

79.

Seymour was already seated, along with his cat, Shadow. But there were two additional places set—one at either end of the table. I sat down at the head of the table (why not?) and began eating the chicken *paprikash* on my plate.

To say it was the best meal I've had since I arrived in Ghastly would be an understatement. This was the best meal I've had in *years*! And I am no stranger to fine restaurants, as you well know.

When I asked the boy where he'd learned to cook a gourmet meal, he laughed and shook his head. "I didn't make it," he whispered, pointing to the unoccupied chair at the other end of table. "*She* did."

Now here's where things started getting interesting. The kid had somehow rigged up a fork that raised and lowered itself onto the plate. And the kicker? This trick fork actually scooped food from the plate and raised it approximately 12 inches. *And then the food disappeared into thin air, as if an invisible mouth were eating!*

It's a clever little trick, wouldn't you say? And it forces me to reevaluate my opinion of this child.

I mean, really, Gadds. How in the world did he do it? I asked Seymour several times, but he just laughed harder and pointed at the empty chair, saying: "Don't ask me. Ask *her*!"

Never mind. I shall use the gimmick somewhere in my book, which I intend to work on tomorrow after I gently reprimand my housemate. The incorrigible brat is downstairs banging on the piano again.

Ignatius

Ignatius B. Grumply

July 7

Seymour Hope
Third floor
43 Old Cemetery Road
Ghastly, Illinois

Seymour:

The sound of you banging on the piano keys
prevented me from working on my book last
night. It is most distracting to have that kind
of noi

*Seymour has informed you that he doesn't
know how to play the piano.*

SEE? This is what I mean. I have no idea how
you're able to access my computer and add a
line of text, but I

It's easy.

All right. You win. Tell me what it will take for
you to leave me alone.

I want to chat with you. About our book.

Our book? Since when are *we* writing a book?

Since I decided to help you. I wasn't going to, given your sourpuss attitude. But I find myself feeling a bit sorry for you, Iggy.

Now wait just a blasted minute. Nobody calls me Iggy except

Your ex-fiancée, Nadia.

What's wrong, Iggy? Cat got your tongue?

How did you know that Nadia called me Iggy?

Because I'm a ghost, you insufferable bore. And because I read your diary.

You wha-wha-*what*?!

I read your diary. Stop sputtering. I'm as old as dirt. Nothing shocks me. Shall I tell you more?

Go ahead. I'm curious.

All right. I know that you're afraid of heights. I know that you hate green peppers and liver. I know that your favorite piece of music is Beethoven's Seventh Symphony. I know that you've been in love only once— with Nadia—and that she broke your heart when she refused to marry you.

She has nothing to do with this! That was 20 years ago. And besides

Stop interrupting. You spent all your money on Nadia—flowers, furs, diamonds, expensive trips to Paris, Milan, Fiji.

Don't forget the cat.

She had a cat?

Don't they all? This one was a Siamese, with a weakness for caviar-flavored cat food and a diamond-studded collar. With emeralds. Stupid cat cost me a fortune. Never mind that. How did you know about Nadia? Not even E. Gadds knows how I lost all my money.

Of course he doesn't know. He's not a ghost. May I continue?

I'm not sure I can stop you.

After Nadia dumped you, you felt ashamed and embarrassed that you had lost your heart and all your money to a woman.

Don't forget the cat. I'm still paying off that blasted collar.

Be quiet. After Nadia dumped you, you thought the only thing to do was to turn off your feelings. But look at you, Iggy. You're deader than I am. And that's why you haven't been able to write a book in 20 years.

I want you to stop this, whoever you are.

I'm Olive C. Spence. And that slight breeze you just felt blow through the room was the sound of me sighing. Why is it so hard for you to believe me?

I don't believe in anything or anyone.

I know you don't, Iggy. But being cynical gets old. Besides that, it's boring. Would you believe in ghosts if we met formally?

What do you mean?

I mean a date. You haven't been on one in years, Iggy.

You want to go on a *date* with me?

Why not? Seymour can be our chaperone.

I knew it. This is Seymour, isn't it? You relentless brat!

I am NOT Seymour. He's cutting Mrs. McCorpse's yard. If you don't believe me, look out the window. Go ahead. Get out of your chair and look out the window. See him? Now wave to him, Iggy. I said, WAVE TO HIM.

How are you doing this? Hey! Stop that!!! Somebody's tickling me. STOP!!! PLE3AS#E ST#&OP TI*CK&&LING ME!!!

Do you still think I'm Seymour?

Stop tickling me!!! PLE&A*SE????? OKAY, OKAY! You're not Seymour!

Thank you. I'll stop tickling now. You have no idea what that child has been through.

Who—Seymour?

I found the letter Seymour's parents left for him while he was sleeping. They told him in their pathetic little note that they weren't "cut out" to be his parents. They said they couldn't have him telling his "silly ghost stories" during their lecture tour. And then they crept out of the house and slinked off to Europe, the wretched weasels. Can you imagine? Just because *they* couldn't see me, they assumed Seymour was lying about the wonderful friendship he and I had established years ago, when he was just a baby.

I had no idea.

Of course you didn't! You were too busy thinking about yourself. You think you're the only person who's ever been rejected. Well, Iggy, let me tell you something. My books were rejected by every publisher from New York to Hong Kong. I know a thing or two about rejection. But neither of us has faced the kind of rejection Seymour has. And did you know his parents have no intention of reclaiming him at the end of the summer?

What?

Remember the contract? *"Whoever rents the property will care for Seymour and his cat, Shadow, for the duration of the rental agreement, and return them both in healthy condition to Les and Diane Hope, if they so request."*

Don't worry. I fully intend to return both the boy and his cat to the parents.

But they're not going to request that you do so. Are you paying attention? Les and Diane Hope are going to leave Seymour and Shadow with you.

For how long?

Who knows? As long as they can get away with it, I suppose. I heard them discussing their plan before they left. They said Seymour would be an embarrassment to them and their years of academic research. Just imagine it, will you?

I can't.

Of course you can't, you pompous old fart. It's unthinkable. But rest assured: Les and Diane Hope are having a most unpleasant time on their lecture tour of Europe.

How do you know?

Oh, let's just say I have friends there who owed me favors.

I'm laughing.

I know, dear. I'm right here.

Is this our date?

Heavens no. I'm still in my bathrobe. We'll have our date on Saturday night.

Okay. Where?

Meet me at my grave.

You've got to be kidding.

I never kid, Iggy. Not about dates, anyway. Eight o'clock on the dot in the cemetery. I'll make dinner and bring you a present.

What should I bring?

Flowers, silly. And a willingness to believe. That's enough for now. Bye.

Wait.

What?

Can Seymour really see you?

Of course he can—when I allow myself to be seen. Are you wondering why you can't see me, too?

Yes.

Because you don't believe in me. Not yet, anyway. Good-bye for now. I must prepare for Saturday night. I haven't been on a date in 109 years.

O.C.S.

Tuesday, July 8

Dear Seymour,

Would you be willing to chaperone
my date with Mr. Grumply on
Saturday night?

Love,

Olive

July 9

Olive,

Now you're going on a <u>date</u> with
Mr. Grumply?!

Why????

—Seymour

O.C.S.

Thursday, July 10

Dear Seymour,

Because he needs a friend. And
because I still feel a tad guilty about
that little chandelier incident.

I'm planning a lovely picnic dinner
for Saturday night. Please meet us
at eight o'clock at my grave. And
bring your sketchpad, dear. I want a
drawing of my first date with
Ignatius—even if my image can't be
captured on paper.

Love,

Olive

This is Mr. Grumply admiring Olive's grave.

This is Mr. Grumply reading Olive's manuscript.

This is Mr. Grumply and Olive.

IGNATIUS B. GRUMPLY

SPECIALIZING IN MYSTERIES, MAYHEM & THE MACABRE

TEMPORARY ADDRESS

43 OLD CEMETERY ROAD   **GHASTLY, ILLINOIS**

July 13
2:30 A.M.

E. Gadds
Attorney-at-Law
188 Madison Avenue
New York, NY 10016

Gadds:

The most extraordinary thing has happened. You'll never believe it! I've been up all night reading a book. *My* book! Well, really Olive's book, but it's based on me and her and . . .

Let me take a deep breath and start over.

I'm living in a house with a young boy and a ghost. Yes, a *real* ghost! Her name is Olive C. Spence. She built this house to write her books but could never find anyone to publish her work—until now. We've agreed to collaborate on a book!

Tell him it was my idea.

Of course! I'm sorry, Olive. Gadds, it was all her idea. Olive's taken what little I'd written of the next Ghost Tamer book and breathed life into it. She thinks we need to scrap the character of Bartholomew Brown and instead use Seymour, Olive, and me. Isn't she brilliant, Gadds? She's already written 100 pages, which she let me read last night by her grave.

Tell him how I didn't let you keep the pages.

She didn't! Just as I was finishing the manuscript, a ferocious wind swept through the cemetery and carried the pages away.

Tell him about Seymour.

Right! The boy is going to illustrate our book. He's a wonderful artist. We've got a long way to go, but it's going to be brilliant. I haven't been this excited about a project in years. Maybe ever!

Well, Gadds, I just wanted to let you know that I'm working with a coauthor. I'm not sure who will get top billing.

Excuse me?

Olive, if you want your name to appear above mine, that's fine. I don't care. I just thought that given my popularity with fans and . . . Never mind. Of course you should have top billing! Good grief, I need to take a deep breath. I should go to bed now. Then in a few hours, I'll wake up, eat a modest breakfast, and start writing what I can *promise* you, Gadds, will be the best book I've ever written!

Cowritten.

Ha! Of course. *Cowritten!* Olive has the whole thing figured out. My role is simply to write her story as best as I can remember it. I've never been so excited in my life! Forget sleep. I'm going to start working on the book right now!

Most enthusiastically yours,

Ignatius

Ignatius B. Grumply

P.S. Will you do me a favor, Gadds, and drop a note to Paige Turner? Tell her the good news. She'll be *thrilled* to hear she's got a future bestseller on her hands!!!

July 18

Ms. Paige Turner
Paige Turner Books
20 West 53rd Street
New York, NY 10019

Dear Ms. Turner,

I owe you an apology.

For months you've been calling my office, asking how Ignatius Grumply was coming along on the next Ghost Tamer book. And for months I've told you that he was just putting the finishing touches on it and would have the completed manuscript to you by August 1.

The sad truth is, he hasn't even started it.

Ignatius has been battling a case of writer's block for years. He would never admit it, of course. But we all knew he was in a slump.

I had hoped his renting a house in the quiet town of Ghastly, Illinois, might jump-start Ignatius's creativity, but it seems to have had the opposite effect. Based on a letter I received from him, I fear Ignatius has gone over the edge.

The letter, written at 2:30 A.M., indicates Ignatius

> 1) believes a ghost is living with him;
>
> 2) thinks he is having "conversations" with this ghost; and
>
> 3) plans to cowrite a book with this ghost, whose name, by the way, is Olive C. Spence.

I realize, Ms. Turner, that this is the last thing you wanted to hear about Ignatius. But I can no longer in good conscience cover for him as I have in the past.

Ignatius is *wigging out*. That's all there is to it.

Regrettably,

E. Gadds

E. Gadds
Attorney-at-Law

Paige Turner
Publisher

July 21

Mr. E. Gadds
Attorney-at-Law
188 Madison Avenue
New York, NY 10016

Dear Mr. Gadds,

Well, this explains why my letters to Ignatius keep coming back marked RETURN TO SENDER/ OCCUPANT HAS LEFT FOR THE SUMMER.

Yes, I knew Ignatius suffered from writer's block. I even knew of his financial problems. I figured if he was broke enough, he'd *have* to write another Ghost Tamer book, whether he wanted to or not.

Like you, I am concerned about Ignatius's mental state. But please understand the terrible public relations implications here. The last thing I want is for young readers across America to find out their favorite author is nuttier than peanut brittle.

Fortunately, I keep a private investigator on my payroll for situations like these. His name is Frank N. Beans. I'm sending him to Ghastly immediately to poke around a bit.

Until we know more details about Ignatius's condition, I suggest we keep this matter to ourselves.

Confidentially yours,

Paige Turner

P.S. I recognize the name Olive C. Spence. Isn't she the woman listed in the *Guinness Book of World Records* for receiving the most rejection slips in history? If memory serves, she wrote something called *graphic epistolary mysteries*—or some such unmarketable nonsense.

➤THE GHASTLY TIMES➤

Friday, July 25
Cliff Hanger, Editor

"Your Secrets Are Our Business"

50 cents
Afternoon Edition

Grumply Grants Interview!

Famous author talks about life, books and his recent victory over writer's block

To celebrate what he calls "the biggest breakthrough" in his life, children's book author Ignatius B. Grumply gave a rare interview yesterday to *The Ghastly Times*.

"I am a new man," proclaimed Grumply, 64, who is spending the summer in Ghastly.

In recent years Grumply, author of 12 books in the Ghost Tamer series, has been famous for what he *wasn't* writing.

"I had a terrible case of writer's block, which I brought on myself," admitted Grumply. "I was miserable, and I was making everyone around me miserable. It's impossible to write when you're selfish and crabby."

What changed his mood?

"It's this new book I'm working on," chirped Grumply. "It's inspired, I tell you!

Ignatius Grumply opens up in a rare interview.

It's brilliant. Finally, I have discovered what true art is! This will be my best book ever!"

Grumply then turned a cartwheel, saying: "I feel 20 years younger!"

Welcome, Frank N. Beans!

Ghastly welcomes Frank N. Beans to town.

Beans, who hails from New Jersey, says he'll be in town a few weeks.

"I'm here on a business trip," said Beans. "It's top secret. I'm investigating the mental state of Ignatius B. Grumply. Wait, you're not going to put this in the newspaper, are you?"

Yes, we are!

(Sorry, Frank. Your secrets are our business!)

Frank N. Beans arrives in Ghastly.

Still No Buyer for Spence Mansion

Demolition is a possibility

If Les and Diane Hope can't find a buyer for Spence Mansion, they might have the 32½-room house demolished and sell the property as an empty lot.

"Of course the sellers would prefer to sell this lovely mansion to someone who can appreciate the, um, history of the house," said real estate agent Anita Sale. "But it *is* a complicated matter, as everyone in Ghastly knows. Demolition is not out of the question."

So far the only person who has expressed interest in buying the house is Seymour Hope, son of Professors Les and Diane Hope.

"Well, it's cute, I suppose," said Sale. "But I hardly think an 11-year-old boy will be able to afford to buy a house with his paper route money."

Spence Mansion, located at 43 Old Cemetery Rd., was once a showplace. Designed and built in 1874 by Olive C. Spence as a place to write her never-published graphic mysteries, the three-story

**If a buyer can't be found,
Spence Mansion might be leveled.**

Victorian home has fallen into disrepair, leading the current owners to conclude that the property might be easier to sell without the house on it.

Professors Les and Diane Hope were not available for comment. The couple is in Europe on a lecture tour to promote the results of a 12-year-long research project, which they hope will conclusively prove that ghosts don't exist.

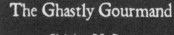

Frank N. Beans

PRIVATE EYE

TO: Paige Turner
RE: Condition of I. B. Grumply
DATE: July 27

REPORT #1

Beans here.

Not much intel to report yet. Did a quick drive-by of 43 Old Cemetery Road. Whatta dump. Imagine three stories of peeling paint and rotten wood with a wrap-around porch that's pulling away from the house, almost like it's scared. Top the whole thing off with a creepy cupola and you've got yourself a real Halloween special.

The house sits at the end of a long dirt road. Ancient oak trees line the drive. There's a cemetery behind the house. The only thing that separates the back-yard of the house from the graveyard is a row of scraggly apple trees—a bit too close for comfort for my taste. Oh yeah, there's also a pond on the west side of the property with a few ducks paddling around.

I saw Grumply. He was taking a walk around the cemetery. Didn't realize how old and flabby he'd gotten. The 11-year-old kid who's living with him was down the block, mowing a neighbor's grass.

The windows of Spence Mansion were open. I think I heard doors slamming inside. Must be the wind.

More to follow in my next report.

Frank N. Beans

Frank N. Beans

P.S. Update: Grumply just went back in the house. I can see him with my binoculars. He's sitting down at his computer.

<u>Book #13 in the Ghost Tamer series</u>

Mystery at Old Cemetery Road:
A New Beginning!

Chapter One

At first, the famous author was skeptical.

Who ever heard of a ghost wanting to col-
laborate on a book with a famous writer like me?
he thought as he admired his handsome reflec-
tion in the mirror.

But it was true. The old ghost who occu-
pied the dusty house he had rented for the summer had made it abundantly clear that she
wanted to help the famous author craft his next
book.

Oh, so I'm an *old* ghost in a *dusty*
house while YOU get to be the famous
author who admires his *handsome* reflec-
tion?

I only meant tha

And I'm *helping* you?

Olive, this is just a first draft.

You didn't even mention me in your interview with *The Ghastly Times*.

I didn't want people to think tha

Forget it. I quit.

July 27

Olive C. Spence
The Cupola
43 Old Cemetery Road
Ghastly, Illinois

Olive:

Are you there?

Please come back so we can continue writing.

Apologetically,

Ignatius

Ignatius

July 28

Olive C. Spence
The Cupola
43 Old Cemetery Road
Ghastly, Illinois

Olive:

I'm sorry. I can be an insensitive clod.

You're not old and I'm not handsome.

And you're not *helping*. You're leading.
You're inspiring.

Repentantly,

Ignatius

Ignatius

July 29

Olive C. Spence
The Cupola
43 Old Cemetery Road
Ghastly, Illinois

Olive:

Can you hear me? Can you read this? Are you in the house? Are you right here in the room?

Please say something. Anything.

Beseechingly,

Ignatius

P.S. Or you could just slam a door or two so I know you're still here. Or play a little something on the piano?

109.

July 30

Seymour Hope
Third floor
43 Old Cemetery Road
Ghastly, Illinois

Seymour:

Do you know where Olive is? I'm afraid
I've made her mad.

What should I do?

Desperately,

I. B. Grumply

Ignatius B. Grumply

July 31

Mr. Grumply,

I have't seen Olive since you guys had your date
in the cemetery.

Sorry.

   —Seymour Hope

P.S. Dang, this means we're on our own for dinner.
If you'll cook tonight, I'll make dinner tomorrow
night.

July 31

Seymour Hope
Third floor
43 Old Cemetery Road
Ghastly, Illinois

Seymour:

Thank you for your response. I would be honored to cook for you tonight. Perhaps a game of checkers after dinner?

And henceforth you may call me Ignatius.

Conciliatorily,

Ignatius

Ignatius

P.S. Olive, if you're reading this, please join Seymour and me for dinner tonight.

Frank N. Beans

TO: Paige Turner
RE: Condition of I. B. Grumply
DATE: July 31

REPORT #2

Beans here.

It's just after nine o'clock P.M. and I'm parked across the street from Spence Mansion. I've been here for an hour or so. Thanks to my binoculars, I can see Grumply and the kid sitting in the dining room. They're eating dinner. Looks like grilled cheese sandwiches.

Grumply keeps getting up and walking around the dining room table. He's a weird bird, all right. He's making wild hand gestures and talking to the walls and the ceiling. The boy just keeps eating. I see a cat sitting at the table. He's eating off a plate. Did I mention the table's set for four? Maybe they were expecting somebody. Well, if they were, nobody came.

But here's something odd: There's a creaky swing on the front porch. You know, one of those old-timey porch swings, like you see in the movies? Well, there's no breeze whatsoever tonight, but the swing is moving back and forth, like somebody's on it.

Whatever. Hardly worth mentioning.

More to follow in my next report.

Frank N. Beans

Frank N. Beans

July 31

Dear Olive,

I'm not sure where you are, but I wanted to say hi.

I had dinner with Mr. Grumply tonight. He's nicer than we thought. He even let Shadow sit at the table and eat with us. After dinner, I let Mr. Grumply beat me at checkers.

Mr. Grumply talked about you all night. He said he never met anyone who could write like you do.

Well, just wanted to tell you that, if you're around.

—Seymour

This is Mr. Grumply trying to work without you.

O.C.S.

Thursday, July 31

Dear Seymour,

Lovely drawing, dear. Thank you.

And yes, I'm here. But don't tell Ignatius. You were right about him from the beginning.

The man is *impossible*! I should've dropped THREE chandeliers on his head.

I refuse to work with that dreadful bore until he starts showing more respect to me *and* to my house. Speaking of which, I just counted your summer earnings. I don't know how you intend to buy my mansion with only $67.50. I suggest you start finding more grass-cutting jobs tomorrow. I'll handle the paper route.

Oh, and if you're wondering why you can't see me, it's because my hair is in curlers at the moment, and I don't feel like being seen—even by you, darling. I may be dead, but I *do* have my pride.

Now go to bed, dear. It's late.

Love,

Olive

July 31

Thanks, Olive!
You're the best.
And I can see
the curlers in
your hair!

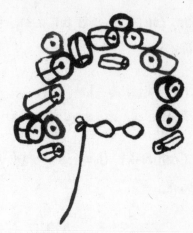

This is you in curlers.

Of course you can
see my curlers.
I can't make all
earthly things
disappear.
But when
you're drawing
a ghost,
you must
remember to
use shadows.
Like this:

Oh, Olive. You're so good at drawing! I wish I could draw like you.

You'll learn—with time and practice. But no more tonight. It's almost midnight.

Okay. Good night, Olive. I'm glad you're still haunting this house.

I gave my word I would for all of eternity—or until one of my books is published. Now go to sleep. The apples in the backyard are ripe. If you work hard this week, I'll make apple tarts, provided I can find a recipe at the library.

You're not going to steal more library books, are you?

I always return what I borrow. (Well, mostly.) Good night, dear.

⮞THE GHASTLY TIMES⮜

"Your Secrets Are Our Business"

Friday, August 1
Cliff Hanger, Editor

50 cents
Afternoon Edition

Hungarian Cookbook Back, but Tart Tomes Taken

M. Balm apologizes for library mess.

A Hungarian cookbook was mysteriously returned to the Ghastly Public Library earlier today.

"I was busy reshelving books," said M. Balm, chief librarian. "Next thing I knew, the missing Hungarian cookbook was in my hand. But then cookbooks were flying off the dessert shelf."

Balm said seven cookbooks devoted to the art of tart baking were taken from the library.

"They just wafted away on their own as if . . . ," began Balm. "Never mind. I don't want to talk about it."

Grumply Grumpy Again

Looks like we spoke too soon.

Children's book author Ignatius B. Grumply is back to his old grumpy self, as evidenced by his rude response to fans who tried to join Grumply on his walk yesterday afternoon.

"I just wanted to say hello and ask him about his new book," said Paul Bearer, a young fan.

"I only wanted to tell him how much I love the Ghost Tamer books," said Sammy Tarry.

But both Bearer and Tarry were given the brush-off by Grumply.

"He said, 'Don't bother me,' " said Bearer.

"To me he said, 'Leave me alone—please,' " said Tarry. "At least he's saying 'please' now."

According to his publisher, Grumply

Grumply's fans are disappointed by his grumpiness.

was supposed to have his next book completed by today. His sour mood suggests he might not have made his deadline.

Spence Mansion Faces Wrecking Ball

Due to their inability to find a buyer for their house, Les and Diane Hope have decided to demolish Spence Mansion and sell the remaining empty lot.

"It was not an easy decision for the Hopes," said Anita Sale, the couple's real estate agent. "But they finally realized they'd have more luck selling an empty lot than a creepy old house, which, let's be honest, is what Spence Mansion is."

Sale said a licensed crew will arrive in Ghastly in a few weeks to prepare for the demolition.

"Ignatius Grumply has a rental contract for the house until September 1," said Sale. "As soon as he leaves, the house will be torn down."

Sale said Les and Diane Hope have decided to remain in Europe.

When asked where Seymour Hope will go after the house is demolished, Sale replied: "The kid's parents told me they're going to pawn him off on Mr. Grumply. I guess the kid can't very well travel with his parents on their lecture tour if he's constantly spouting off about his best friend Olive, the ghost. And Grumply *did* author-

The 134-year-old Spence Mansion will be demolished next month.

ize his lawyer to sign a contract in which Grumply agrees to return Seymour to his parents if they request. And if they don't want him back? Well, Grumply's stuck with the kid and his cat. But Professors Les and Diane Hope don't want anyone to know their plans. So don't print any of this in the newspaper, OK?"

(Sorry, Anita! Your secrets are, well, you know…)

Welcome, Anita Sale!

Ghastly welcomes Anita Sale to town.

Sale is the owner of Proper Properties, a real estate agency based in San Francisco that specializes in unique homes and apartments.

While in Ghastly, Anita will stay at the Ghastly Inn.

Welcome to our town, Anita!

Anita Sale arrives in Ghastly.

Frank N. Beans

PRIVATE EYE

TO: Paige Turner
RE: Condition of I. B. Grumply
DATE: August 2

REPORT #3

Beans here.

It's four o'clock P.M. and I'm reporting from a branch of an apple tree outside Spence Mansion. I can see Grumply through my binoculars. He's sitting in front of his computer, talking to a blank screen. Poor slob. He's got it bad, whatever it is. If he were any other guy, I'd say it was woman problems. But I've been watching Grumply for a week now, and I can confirm there's not a dame alive who would like this guy.

He's standing up now and looking out the window in this direction, toward the cemetery. His lips are moving, like he's talking to somebody. Now he's pointing at the apple tree next to the one I'm sitting in. There's a basket under it. What the heck? An apple just fell from the tree directly into the basket. There goes another one! Two more! It's almost like someone's picking apples and putting them in a basket. Except no one's there.

Wait! Now the basket is floating back to the house.

I'm in my car now. Not sure what that apple thing was all about.

I'm parked in front of the house. The kid is down the street, mowing yards. This is usually the time of day he delivers the afternoon newspaper, but . . . Holy cats. A newspaper just flew onto the front porch of Spence Mansion and landed with a thud. Same thing's happening next door. And the next house, too! Self-propelled newspapers are delivering themselves down the street. What the Sam heck?

I'm outta here. Get somebody else to cover this freak show.

Frank N. Beans

Frank N. Beans

20 West 53rd Street
New York, NY 10019

Paige Turner
Publisher

August 4

Mr. E. Gadds
Attorney-at-Law
188 Madison Avenue
New York, NY 10016

Dear Mr. Gadds,

I am writing to inform you that I have decided to terminate my professional relationship with your client, Ignatius Grumply, due to his

    a) unstable mental condition, and
    b) inability to finish writing the next
       Ghost Tamer book.

I am legally entitled to ask Grumply to return the $100,000 we paid him in advance for the book he never wrote, but I am not going to. Why? Because I'd like to keep this matter as quiet as possible—and also because I know Ignatius has spent the money. I'll just chalk it up to a business loss.

123.

Will you please inform Ignatius of my decision?

Paige Turner

August 7

Ms. Paige Turner
Paige Turner Books
20 West 53rd Street
New York, NY 10019

Dear Ms. Turner,

Your offer to forgive the $100,000 advance is very
generous. I will let Ignatius know.

I will also draw up a termination contract and sign
on behalf of Ignatius. I handle all such paperwork
for him.

I'm sure Ignatius will be disappointed to learn that
his publishing career is over. But I suspect he'll
also be relieved. Ignatius hasn't written anything
worth reading in 20 years. It's time he finally
stopped trying.

Sincerely,

E. Gadds

E. Gadds

125.

AGREEMENT TO TERMINATE
THE CONTRACTUAL RELATIONSHIP BETWEEN

PAIGE TURNER BOOKS

AND

IGNATIUS B. GRUMPLY

This agreement shall end the long-term professional
relationship between
Paige Turner Books and Ignatius B. Grumply.

From now on, anything Grumply writes
or attempts to write
or says he is writing
or will write
is his business.

Paige Turner Books has no interest in Grumply's work
today, tomorrow, and/or forever.

Paige Turner

—————————————————
Paige Turner
for PAIGE TURNER BOOKS

E. Gadds

—————————————————
E. Gadds
for IGNATIUS B. GRUMPLY

August 8

Ignatius B. Grumply
43 Old Cemetery Road
Ghastly, Illinois

Dear Ignatius,

There's no easy way to tell you this, so I'll just be direct. Paige Turner has dumped you.

The good news is, Ms. Turner says she doesn't expect you to return the advance. (Lucky for you, considering there's nothing left.) She's simply going to write off the $100,000 as a business loss.

I'm also writing off the money you owe me. But in doing so, I too must sever my professional ties with you. It's not fair to my other clients who pay for my services. I hope you understand.

Take care of yourself, Ignatius.

So long.

E. Gadds

E. Gadds

P.S. Your landlord in Chicago called me yesterday. He says you're six months behind in your
rent. He's found another tenant for apartment
2-B. Sorry, Ignatius, but you'll have to find somewhere else to live.

IGNATIUS B. GRUMPLY

SPECIALIZING IN MYSTERIES, MAYHEM & THE MACABRE

TEMPORARY ADDRESS

43 OLD CEMETERY ROAD   GHASTLY, ILLINOIS

August 11

E. Gadds
Attorney-at-Law
188 Madison Avenue
New York, NY 10016

Gadds:

Believe it or not, I understand completely.
I don't blame you or Paige Turner one bit.
Your only mistake was waiting so long to
do this.

Finally,

Ignatius

Ignatius

UNTITLED

The man was old and creaky. Bald, too. Overweight. And a complete failure.

At one time in his life, he had been a halfway decent writer. But that was long ago. Now he couldn't write to save his life. He often wondered why. The more he wondered, the less he could write at all. He was stuck.

Then the writer met a woman. She explained what his problem was: selfishness.

The man knew she was right. His inability to care about anyone other than himself had made him a lousy writer and a miserable man.

Realizing this was painful for the writer. But in an odd way it felt good, too, because he suddenly found himself caring about this woman who had told him the truth about himself. It felt strange to know that there could exist a person who knew him as well as this woman did. It made him feel something he hadn't felt in many years.

But what did the writer do? He blew it. His inflated ego got the best of him. He was try-ing to be a big shot, a VIP. Very Important

Person. More like a Very Insufferable Pig.

Now you're being too hard on yourself.

Olive! Is that you?

Who else talks to you like this?

I can't tell you how relieved I am.

I'm not wearing my glasses. Do I see the word *exist* on the previous page?

Yes! I'll retype it in a bigger font. I wrote: *It felt strange to know that there could exist a person*

I have my glasses now. Move your head so I can read the rest.

Olive. Please stay.

You're inviting me to stay in my own house? Hardly necessary, Iggy.

What I mean is, I want to try again. Please? Will you write a book with me?

Why should I?

I've changed. I've grown. I've learned something about myself and others.

Aha! Character development. Very important in a story.

I'm not talking about a character or a story. I'm talking about me.

I know. But we're all characters in our own stories, Iggy. You're frowning.

I'm not sure I understand.

All I'm saying is that your life *is* a story, and that you are the main character of that story. Is your story a comedy or a tragedy? Is it dull? Or is it a compelling, spine-tingling drama? My point, Iggy, is simply that each of us is the author of his or her own life. So if you're telling me that you've changed, I'm pleased at your authorship.

Does this mean you'll stay and write a book with me?

Oh, I suppose we could try. Iggy, what is it? You look like you've seen a ghost.

For a minute there I thought I saw . . . Olive, is that you?

Of course it's me. Didn't anyone ever tell you it's rude to stare? Now scoot over, dear. I write better when I'm sitting down.

⇒THE GHASTLY TIMES⇐

Sunday, August 17
Cliff Hanger, Editor

"Your Secrets Are Our Business"

$1.50
☀ Morning Edition

Demolition Crew Prepares to Level Spence Mansion

A ... ... ansion.
crew ... ... as an
Gha ... ... r than
night ... ... ooky
plans ... ... Sale,
ing ... ... g to
Mansic ... ... half
Ac ... ... he
to rea ... ... se
agent Ar ... ... g
the 134- ... ... r
mansion ... ...
at 43 ... ...
Cemetery ... ...
will be c ... ... nsion are
ished as soo ... ... Hope, their son Seymour
"Les an ... ... and Ignatius B. Grumply, who is renting the
they'll have ... ... selling the mansion for the summer.

Dear Subscriber,

With today's edition of the newspaper, you are also receiving the first three chapters of a true ghost story called *43 Old Cemetery Road*. We hope you like it.

If you're interested in reading the next three chapters, please send $3 to:

43 Old Cemetery Road
Ghastly, Illinois

We plan to keep writing, illustrating, and publishing additional chapters for as long as readers are interested.

Sincerely,

O.C.S.
Olive C. Spence
Coauthor

Ignatius B. Grumply
Ignatius B. Grumply
Coauthor

Seymour
Seymour Hope
Illustrator

August 27

Ms. Anita Sale
c/o The Ghastly Inn
99 Coffin Avenue
Ghastly, Illinois

Ms. Sale:

I am writing with two requests.

First, I ask that you please accept my apology for the rude letters I wrote to you earlier this summer. I was a pompous bore, but I have since changed my ways.

Second, I am asking you to inform Les and Diane Hope that a buyer has been found for Spence Mansion. The buyer is a current occupant of the house, who requests that you cancel the demolition order.

Enclosed please find a check for $250,000.

Thank you.

Sincerely,

I. B. Grumply

Ignatius B. Grumply

August 28

Mr. Ignatius B. Grumply
43 Old Cemetery Road
Ghastly, Illinois

Dear Mr. Grumply,

An enthusiastic YES to both requests. I am calling Mr. and Mrs. Hope right now. They will be thrilled by the news!

Congratulations on your new house!

Anita Sale

Anita Sale

Hôtel de Sens
1, rue du Figuier
Paris, France

August 29

Seymour Hope
43 Old Cemetery Road
Ghastly, Illinois   USA

INTERNATIONAL
OVERNIGHT MAIL

Dear Seymour,

Have you heard the good news? Anita Sale has found a buyer for our house! We're so proud of you for not scaring off Mr. Grumply with those silly ghost stories!

Ms. Sale also tells us you've become VERY rich this summer. What a smart boy! Don't worry about the money. We can convert it to euros when we return to Europe with you.

We'll be home soon to finalize the sale and pick you up!

Sincerely,

Mom + Dad

P.S. Sorry we haven't had a chance to write before now. We've missed you so much!

137.

August 30

Professors Les and Diane Hope
c/o Hôtel de Sens
1, rue du Figuier
Paris, France

Dear Mom and Dad,

You're right that Anita Sale found a buyer for 43
Old Cemetery Road. It's me.

I bought the house with the help of Mr. Grumply and
Olive C. Spence. We're going to live here together.

You're right about something else, too. Remember that
letter you left for me when you snuck off to Europe
in the middle of the night? You wrote that you're not
cut out to be my parents. I agree.

Good luck in Paris and in life.

Sincerely,

    —Seymour Hope

Your former son

Sunday, August 31

Seymour Hope and Ignatius B. Grumply
43 Old Cemetery Road
Ghastly, Illinois

Dearest Seymour and Ignatius,

Orders for more chapters of *43 Old Cemetery Road* are coming in from all over the world! I just counted our funds to date. After giving Seymour enough money to buy this house, we still have $350,000.

And that's just the beginning! The more chapters you write (Ignatius) and illustrate (Seymour), the more money you'll make.

Isn't it exciting? Just think: Ignatius overcame his writer's block. Seymour was able to buy the house he loved. And *I* published a book. Well, *co*-published a book, but still . . . I did it! Or rather, *we* did it!

And even more amazing, people in town are starting to believe in me. I was just down at the Ghastly Gourmand picking up some muffins when I heard Shirley U. Jest telling her customers, "I don't care if a ghost *did* help write it. *43 Old Cemetery Road* is the best ghost story I've ever read. I can't wait to read the rest of it!"

It's music to my ears, boys. Music to my ears . . . And do you know the best part of all? I don't have to haunt this old house anymore. I can finally retire to my grave and rest in peace. You have no idea how exhausting this haunting business is.

A few things before I go:

Ignatius, may I suggest that you use $100,000 from our book fund to repay Paige Turner the money she advanced you on that silly Ghost Tamer book? I also think you should send E. Gadds $3,000 for the summer rental of my house and $10,000 to cover your legal bills. You'll just feel better about yourself if you do, Iggy.

Seymour, I want you to use as much money as you need to turn the third floor into an artist's studio.

As for me, I'd like someone to keep my grave tidy. Flowers are nice but not necessary. I know you two will be busy with your publishing careers. Just remember me. That's all I really want. And be kind to each other. Remember that other people are as real as you. Other people's feelings are as real as yours. In fact, our feelings are what *make* us real.

I'm glad you two have each other. Enjoy my house. I know you'll take good care of it—and each other.

Better sign off before I become a weepy mess.

Good-bye forever.

Love,

Olive

August 31

Dear Olive,

Don't go. This house wouldn't be the same
without you.

I don't want to live in your mansion if you're
not here.

Please stay . . . forever.

Love,
　 —Seymour

This is me (and Shadow) begging you to stay.

IGNATIUS B. GRUMPLY

A WORK IN PROGRESS

PERMANENT ADDRESS

43 OLD CEMETERY ROAD   GHASTLY, ILLINOIS

August 31

Olive C. Spence
The Cupola
43 Old Cemetery Road
Ghastly, Illinois

Dear Olive,

When I moved into your house, I thought I'd
made a terrible mistake. The last thing I wanted
was an 11-year-old boy and his cat to babysit for
the summer.

But Olive, you showed me what it means to care
for someone again. And now, like you, I *care*
about Seymour. I really do! For a kid, he's not
bad at all. I'm even growing a bit fond of that
furball cat of his. So what if Shadow makes me
sneeze? I'll buy more handkerchiefs. I'll buy a
truckload of handkerchiefs!

And . . . well, how should I describe my feelings
for you? I like that you slam doors when you're
mad. I like that you made sure Les and Diane

144.

Hope (the rats!) had a miserable summer in Europe. I like how protective you are of Seymour. I like how you read over my shoulder when I'm trying to work. I like how you make me excited about writing and life.

I find myself thinking about you all the time and wondering if what I feel could be *love*. I don't care if that sounds crazy. It's how I feel.

I feel. I don't think I've ever written that and meant it—*really* meant it—in my life. You've taught me how to feel. You believed in me. How could I not believe in you?

And you were right. I *was* dead before I met you. Now I'm alive because of you.

I could say more, but why? What I'm trying to express is very simple. I've fallen in love with you, Olive C. Spence. Please don't leave me now.

Love,

Iggy

P.S. And if that doesn't work, I'm not above playing the guilt card. Stay for Seymour's sake.

Please, Olive, the boy needs a mother, and he adores you. Stay for his sake, if not for mine.

P.P.S. Of course I hope you'll stay for both Seymour *and* me. But now I'm rambling like an old fool.

P.P.P.S. Okay, I'll just say it: You, me, and Seymour. Couldn't we be our own kind of family?

O.C.S.

Monday, September 1

Dearest Seymour and Ignatius,

Okay, you silly boys. I'll stay. But only
if you both promise to do your share of
the work around here.

Let's celebrate with a fancy dinner
tonight. I'll cook. Iggy, you can do the
dishes. And Seymour, I'd like you to
paint a formal portrait of us.

Till eight o'clock—

Yours in the cupola,

Olive

P.S. It's nice to be wanted. Thank you,
my dears.

147.

This is me with my new family.

And so, we end with a beginning.

Because every ending is really a beginning.

All you need is a house that's old and creaky . . .

filled with lots of books . . .

a cat . . .

a person who's willing to try again . . .

someone who
promises to never
leave . . .

and most important of all . . .

a little Hope.

Nice touch, Olive.

Thank you, Iggy.

The End

(for now . . .)

HOUSE Your Knowledge

A laundry chute delivers dirty clothes and linens from upper floors to the basement laundry.

An ice box, used in the days before refrigeration, kept food cold with a block of ice.

A dumbwaiter is a small elevator used to move food and drink (and sometimes surprises) from one floor to another.

A newel is the upright post at the base of a staircase.

A transom is a hinged window above a door that can be used to let in light or air.